✳ Smithsonian

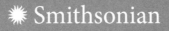

A STAR LIKE
JESSE OWENS

BY NIKKI SHANNON SMITH

ILLUSTRATED BY LISA MANUZAK WILEY

STONE ARCH BOOKS
a capstone imprint

A Star Like Jesse Owens is published by Stone Arch Books,
an imprint of Capstone.

1710 Roe Crest Drive
North Mankato, Minnesota 56003
www.capstonepub.com

The name of the Smithsonian Institution and the sunburst logo
are registered trademarks of the Smithsonian Institution. For more
information, please visit www.si.edu.

Library of Congress Cataloging-in-Publication Data is available on
the Library of Congress website.
ISBN: 978-1-4965-9861-5 (hardcover)
ISBN: 978-1-4965-9869-1 (paperback)
ISBN: 978-1-4965-9865-3 (ebook PDF)

Summary:

Matthew is an African American boy who dreams of becoming an
Olympic runner like his hero, Jesse Owens. But there's a problem.
Matthew has asthma, which makes it hard for him to run. When
his journalist father is assigned to cover the 1936 Olympics
in Germany, Matthew jumps at the chance to tag along. Will
Owens's amazing Olympic victories inspire Matthew in his own
chosen career? Find out in this historical fiction series created in
partnership with the Smithsonian. Real-world facts combine with
#ownvoices stories to bring American history to vivid life.

Designer: Tracy McCabe

Our very special thanks to Megan Smith, Senior Creative
Developer, Officer of Audience Engagement, National Museum of
American History, Smithsonian. Capstone would also like to thank
Kealy Gordon, Product Development Manager, and the following
at Smithsonian Enterprises: Jill Corcoran, Director, Licensed
Publishing; Brigid Ferraro, Vice President, Education and Consumer
Products; and Carol LeBlanc, President, Smithsonian Enterprises.

Printed in the United States of America.
PA117

TABLE OF CONTENTS

Chapter 1

The Luckiest Boy in Ohio

July 15, 1936
The SS *Manhattan*, New York, U.S.A.

Matthew held on tight to the rail of the deck. He'd never been on a boat before—not even a rowboat. In fact, Matthew stayed close to home most of the time. Now, here he was, aboard a luxury liner headed to Germany. His daddy stood next to him, one arm around Matthew's shoulders.

Matthew watched New York City get smaller and smaller as the ship sailed away.

Then he turned his attention to the people on the boat. They were everywhere, packed so closely together on the deck that Matthew could barely move. Some of them were still waving goodbye to people who had come to see them off. Some were laughing and yelling. Others stood nervously on deck like they didn't know what to do.

A lot of the passengers were holding tiny American flags. To Matthew, it seemed like the ship was a small floating version of the United States. The SS *Manhattan* was the biggest ocean liner the nation had ever built. It was painted red, white, and blue. A big flag with the Olympic rings on it waved in the cool breeze.

"Daddy," said Matthew, "are all these people going to the Olympics?"

"I don't know, son," said Daddy.

Matthew smiled up at his father. Daddy was the founder of the *Afro-American Voice*, a newspaper back home in Ohio. He was going to the Olympics so he could write about it. Matthew got to go too, which made him the luckiest boy in Ohio.

"How you feeling, son?" asked Daddy.

Matthew knew why Daddy was asking. There had been a lot of disagreement in their house about Matthew going to Germany. Mama hadn't wanted to let him go. She didn't want to let Matthew go anywhere because he was what she called *sickly*. Mama was always worried Matthew would have an asthma attack and maybe even die.

"I feel good," said Matthew. He wasn't really lying. The excitement was making it a little hard to breathe, but Matthew often had trouble breathing. He was not going to let his asthma ruin a once-in-a-lifetime opportunity. He had already decided to say he was fine every single time Daddy asked.

But just then the cool breeze brushed past Matthew's face. Several tight coughs gave the truth away.

"The sun's setting, and it's getting cold," Daddy said, turning to him with concern. "Let's go have dinner and turn in."

***

July 16, 1936
The SS *Manhattan*, Atlantic Ocean

The next morning before breakfast, Daddy took Matthew onto the promenade deck of the ship for some fresh air. Matthew couldn't believe his eyes. The passengers on deck weren't all just passengers. They were athletes, and they were *everywhere*! Matthew hadn't noticed them yesterday in the crowd. There were gymnasts practicing on bars, weightlifters lifting weights, and boxers sparring.

There was a swimming pool right on the ship too, full of swimmers. Matthew thought it looked more like a gymnasium than a big ship.

"Daddy, are these the Olympic athletes?" Matthew whispered.

Matthew's father chuckled. "Sure are," he said. "All the American athletes are on this ship. We'll be traveling on the same deck with them."

That means Jesse Owens is here somewhere! Matthew thought. His eyes darted around, searching for his hero.

If Matthew could be like anyone in the whole world, it would be Jesse Owens. Jesse lived in Ohio too. He was a college student at Ohio State University. He ran for the Ohio Buckeyes track team. Now he was going to run in the Olympics, and Matthew wanted Jesse to win.

"Daddy," said Matthew, "can we go find the track team?" Matthew's dream was to be a track star one day. For now, he'd have to settle for running on the sidewalk in front of his house.

Daddy winked. "Stay close to me," he said.

Matthew followed his father. He wondered if the ship had a track too. Matthew peeked through the spaces between the people crowded on deck to try to catch a glimpse of Jesse Owens. But Matthew couldn't see him anywhere.

Suddenly, shouts rang out, followed by cheers and clapping. In the distance, Matthew noticed a crowd of people watching something. He couldn't see what it was, but Daddy grabbed Matthew's hand and pushed their way to the front.

There he was—*Jesse Owens!* He was showing the crowd how fast he was. Jesse was

dressed in a suit like the one Matthew's daddy wore to church, even though he was on a boat. And running.

Jesse sped down the deck toward a pole held by two men in the crowd. *Whoosh!* He cleared the hurdle like it was nothing.

Another cheer filled the air. No fancy suit was going to slow down Jesse Owens. Jesse turned around and raced back toward Matthew and his father.

Matthew held his breath as the great Jesse got closer and closer. His heart thudded in his ears like he was the one running.

Jesse flew over the pole again. Matthew could see why they called him the Buckeye Bullet. To Matthew, Jesse looked faster than a bullet.

Daddy shook Matthew's shoulder. "Son, you okay?" he asked.

"Huh?" said Matthew.

"Son, you look pale. Breathe," said Daddy. "You're not breathing. Are you having an asthma attack?"

Matthew laughed and exhaled. He was so excited he'd forgotten to breathe. "No, Daddy! I'm not having an attack," said Matthew. "Did you see Jesse go?"

"Yes, indeed," said Daddy.

Daddy had been covering Jesse Owens's events at Ohio State University for the past year. He had even interviewed Jesse. Matthew had read every single article too. He knew Jesse Owens used to have trouble breathing when he was little, just like Matthew did. But Jesse was fine now—better than fine. He was the fastest man in the world! And he was a Negro!

One day, I'll be fast. They'll call me the next Buckeye Bullet, thought Matthew.

Jesse noticed Matthew's father in the

crowd and nodded at him. Then he looked at Matthew and winked. Matthew grinned and clapped as hard as he could. When he was done, his hands hurt.

Soon it was time for breakfast. The dining room was full of athletes. Matthew and his father sat at a table in the corner.

"Are you watching people?" asked Matthew.

Daddy always watched people. He said observing and asking the right questions helped him write articles with heart. When he'd started the *Afro-American Voice*, Daddy had been the only reporter. Then he'd hired a few people and became the top reporter. Now he only took the stories he thought were the most important.

Daddy put a forkful of eggs in his mouth and nodded his head. "Watching and listening," he said.

Matthew ate his breakfast and pretended he was a reporter like his father. He noticed that a man at the next table looked seasick and wasn't eating anything.

One of the other men at the next table asked the others, "What do you think Germany will be like?"

"I've heard Germany is a mess right now. Full of hate aimed at the Jewish people," said his friend. "Plus, I'm worried about Hitler."

Matthew stopped chewing so he could hear what they said. Daddy had told him about Adolf Hitler. Hitler was the leader of Germany and the Nazis. Matthew's father didn't like Hitler or the Nazis. He said they wanted to get rid of all the Jewish people. Matthew had been too scared to ask Daddy how they would do that.

Another man at the table spoke up. "Germany can't be worse than America.

America's full of hate too," he said. "It's aimed at the Negroes, though."

Matthew looked at his father. Daddy was sipping coffee and looking at his plate. Matthew knew he was listening to the same conversation.

The first man said, "There was a lot of talk about the American teams boycotting the Olympics."

A Negro man at the end of the table spoke quietly. "I thought about not coming," he said. "God knows I can't stand racism. I face discrimination every single day at home. But it's the Olympics. I can't think of a better way to prove I'm just as good as anyone else. I'll show 'em. Germany *and* America."

"I sure hope the Nazis don't target *you*," said the man next to him. "They don't just hate Jews. They hate everyone who isn't white and Aryan."

The Negro man shook his head sadly. "I just don't understand the Aryan thing. It's a mystery to me why they think blond hair and blue eyes could possibly make one person better than the next."

The table fell silent, and Daddy stood up. Matthew wiped his mouth and followed his father out of the dining room. Matthew didn't say a word until they got back to their room.

"Daddy," Matthew said after his father closed the door, "Who's worse? Germany or America?"

Matthew's father thought for a long time. Finally he said, "I don't know, son. I just don't know."

Matthew's chest felt tight. He breathed in deeper, trying to get enough air. Daddy hadn't told Matthew the United States had considered a boycott. That meant Hitler was even worse than Matthew had realized. *What if the Germans* did *target them?* he thought.

Matthew tried hard to push his worries about Germany to the back of his mind. He'd know soon enough what Germany was like.

Chapter 2

The Games Begin

August 1, 1936
Olympic Stadium, Berlin, Germany

Matthew's heart thumped as the Olympic torch was lit. He felt like all the energy of the crowd was pumping through his veins. Not even the rain could dampen his spirits. This was the moment he had been waiting for.

The teams paraded into the stadium. Matthew could see *everything* from the press box. He watched each country's team lower its flag as they passed by. It looked like the flags were bowing.

"Daddy," whispered Matthew, "why are they doing that with the flags?"

"It's a show of respect to the host," Daddy whispered back.

Matthew's eyes got big. "To Hitler?" he asked in a voice so quiet it barely came out.

Matthew's father nodded and pointed to a box not too far away. Matthew recognized Hitler's face immediately because his picture was always in newspapers. Matthew quickly turned his eyes back to the parade. He recognized the American team as soon as he spotted the red, white, and blue. That meant Jesse Owens would march past them soon.

Matthew stood on his toes so he wouldn't miss Jesse. The American team got closer and closer. At the spot where the other teams dipped their flags, the Americans didn't. The American flag waved high and proud.

Good, thought Matthew. *If Hitler is prejudiced, he doesn't deserve their respect.*

But then he had another thought. *What if Hitler gets mad at America?*

***

August 3, 1936
Olympic Stadium, Berlin, Germany

The rain fell onto the track. Matthew had hoped it would stop in time for Jesse Owens's first event. Matthew didn't want Jesse to fall or run too slowly because he couldn't get good traction. He worried the track would be too slippery for the one-hundred-meter dash. That was about the length of a football field. There was no time for mistakes. The race would probably only take fifteen seconds.

Daddy had told Matthew what to expect for today's race. Matthew's father had never been to an Olympics before either, but he had learned as much as he could before they left. He wanted to understand it so his articles would make people feel like they were there.

Jesse would be competing against one of the German runners. His name was Erich Borchmeyer. Matthew knew Hitler would be rooting for his own country's runner. But he wondered how Hitler would feel if Jesse won—not just an American, but a Negro.

"Win, Jesse," Matthew said under his breath. He wished he could run in the race too. He wouldn't even care if Jesse beat him.

Jesse took his place in lane two. Matthew's heart sped up. "Go, Jesse. You can do it," he whispered.

Matthew's father grinned at him. "Here we go," he said.

The starter's gun went off, and Matthew jumped from the sound. The runners took off! Jesse's feet hit the ground as fast as Matthew's heart thumped in his chest. Matthew imagined that his heartbeat was the sound of his own feet pounding. In his mind, he ran right next to Jesse.

Jesse was faster than the rest of the runners, but it was close. Matthew clapped and jumped up and down. Jesse was going to win. He just knew it.

The race was over almost as fast as it had started. Jesse won first place in just a little more than ten seconds. The other runners were right behind him.

As Jesse crossed the finish line, it sounded like every single person in the stadium was cheering. They didn't sound mad at all. They were *impressed*. The stadium was erupting with noise! Jesse was so good he had the whole world cheering for him.

Matthew glanced at Hitler. He couldn't believe his eyes. *Hitler saluted.*

Now Matthew wanted to be like Jesse more than ever.

Jesse Owens had won the gold *and* tied a world record at the same time. The American flag was raised and music started. They were playing "The Star Spangled Banner" for Jesse. Cameras were flashing everywhere.

Matthew watched Hitler as Jesse walked by. Yesterday, Hitler had invited athletes to his box so he could congratulate them, but he had stopped doing that. Matthew had a feeling Hitler didn't want to shake hands with Negroes who won.

Anger flashed inside Matthew for just a minute, but then it disappeared. *Hitler is a sore loser,* he thought.

Nothing could take away Jesse Owens's gold medal. Matthew looked up at his father. He was jumping and whooping and trying to write in his notebook at the same time.

Matthew grinned and whooped even louder.

Daddy sure was going to have some good news to write about. Matthew wondered if he would write about Hitler deciding to quit shaking hands in the article too.

As the crowd quieted, Matthew realized he was wheezing. Jumping and yelling was making his asthma flare up.

I'd better take it easy so I don't miss any of the games, Matthew thought. The last thing he wanted was to spend tomorrow in his hotel room inhaling medicated vapors.

Chapter 3

Trouble

August 4, 1936
Olympic Stadium, Berlin, Germany

Matthew stood in the stands, trying to figure out what was going on. Jesse Owens was stretching, and there were a lot of runners down on the track. An announcer said, "It's time for the two-hundred-meter heat!"

"Daddy, what's a heat?" asked Matthew. He had heard the word before, but wasn't sure what it meant.

"Officials set up heats when there are too many runners to be on the track at one time," explained Daddy. "They break the runners into small groups to compete in races. The races are called heats. The officials record everyone's time. Then at the end, the fastest runner from each heat will run in the finals."

Matthew frowned and asked, "So, it's a way to eliminate runners?"

Daddy smiled and said, "Exactly. In the end, a few will rise above the rest."

"I know Jesse Owens will rise above the rest!" exclaimed Matthew.

A few of the other reporters in the press box chuckled. Daddy put a finger to his lips to remind Matthew not to talk so loud. Matthew glanced around and nodded. Not everyone would agree with what he'd said about Jesse—or find it funny.

He wasn't joking about Jesse rising to the top, though. Jesse just *had* to win the heat, so that he could move on to the long jump.

Sometimes, when Matthew felt good, he would go outside and pretend he was a track star. He liked to practice the long jump because it was easiest for him. There wasn't too much running. He'd use the lines and cracks on the sidewalk as markers. He'd take a running start, jump, and then look at what crack he'd landed on. Then he'd do it again and try to jump farther.

The only problem was Mama. She was always telling Matthew to slow down or be careful or come inside before he had an attack. Matthew didn't care if he wheezed. How was he supposed to get better if he didn't practice?

Sometimes Matthew heard Daddy say, "Louise, let that boy be. He'll be okay."

Then Mama would say, "You aren't the one who stays home worrying on the bad days, Malcolm. I am."

After a while, Daddy would call Matthew inside. One of these days, though, Matthew wasn't going to have anybody calling him in. One of these days, the voices would be calling, "Matthew! Matthew! Matthew!" He'd be far ahead of the other runners while the crowd cheered—just as they did for Jesse.

The sound of the starter gun snapped Matthew out of his daydream. The heats started, and Matthew saw he was right. Jesse Owens *definitely* rose above the rest.

Jesse would get to compete in the finals for the two-hundred-meter race, but that wasn't until tomorrow. Matthew would have to wait to see what happened.

Finally, it was time for the long jump.

Matthew was so nervous it felt like he was the one competing. All the muscles in his body tensed.

Jesse would have three tries to make it to the finals. Matthew wasn't worried that Jesse wouldn't qualify. Jesse had already broken the long jump world record last year at the Big Ten Championships. He was a shoo-in.

The officials raised their flags to signal the beginning of the competition. But when the flags dropped, Matthew's breath caught in his throat. *Jesse messed up.* He did a warm-up jump instead of a real jump, and the officials said it counted as his real jump!

"Daddy, can't they let him have a do-over?" Matthew wondered.

Daddy shook his head sadly. Matthew crossed his fingers and waited for the next jump. He could hear himself wheezing, but in his mind he *became* Jesse Owens.

Matthew kept his eyes on the officials. He waited for the flags. This time at the signal, Jesse jumped. In the stands, Matthew jumped too. But Jesse fouled! His foot was too far forward.

Matthew hung his head. He and Jesse only had one chance left. If they messed up again, they wouldn't even qualify for the final jump.

Daddy shook Matthew's shoulder. "Matthew," he said. "Son, breathe."

Matthew looked up at his father. He realized his wheezing had gotten louder. He was struggling to inhale. This was how his asthma attacks usually started. Matthew knew if his breathing got any worse, Daddy would make him leave. But there was no way Matthew was leaving the stadium until the long jump was over.

Daddy reached into his pocket and pulled out a small jar. Matthew knew right away

what it was, and he wasn't happy about it. It was one of Mama's potions. She had sent a few jars with them to Germany.

Matthew hated Mama's potions. They were full of ingredients that weren't meant to go together: oregano, garlic, ginger, and who knew what else. They were disgusting, even though Mama put honey in them to help with the taste.

One time Mama had made it so strong that Matthew spat it out in the sink. Mama hadn't liked that very much, but Matthew thought he'd heard Daddy chuckle.

Daddy held the open jar out toward Matthew. "Drink it," he said.

Matthew shook his head and pressed his lips together, which made breathing even harder.

"Drink it, or we leave," threatened Daddy.

The announcer's voice blared over the speaker. "One more chance for Jesse Owens!"

Matthew grabbed the jar, drank the potion, and handed the empty jar back to Daddy. He didn't know if Daddy would really leave, but it was possible. Matthew forced himself to pretend he was better. He didn't have a choice.

Daddy stared at Matthew, who worked hard to make his breathing look easy. Matthew turned his eyes back to the track. He breathed and said a little prayer for Jesse.

Chapter 4

Surprises

August 4, 1936
Olympic Stadium, Berlin, Germany

Jesse Owens took his place to get ready for his last jump.

Jesse put one foot back. So did Matthew. Jesse crouched slightly and spread out his fingers. Matthew did too. Then Jesse took off. He ran the short distance toward the sand and leaped.

"*Whoosh*," whispered Matthew.

Jesse landed, and the officials measured the

43

distance—more than 7.15 meters. Jesse had qualified! Matthew jumped up and down and hollered until he felt his father's hand on his shoulder.

"Take it easy, Matthew," Daddy warned. "Why don't you sit down for a while?"

Matthew didn't want to push his luck. He sat down until it was time for the real long jump competition. Then he was right back on his feet.

The final competition was between Jesse Owens and Luz Long—the United States against Germany. Each time one man jumped, the other jumped farther.

To Matthew's surprise, the crowd chanted, "U.S.A.! U.S.A.!"

Jesse took off for his final jump. It was like he was trying to fly right out of the stadium. Matthew thought maybe Jesse was trying to jump all the way home to America.

When Jesse landed, the cheers exploded from the crowd again.

"Eight point oh six meters," said the announcer. "A new Olympic record and a second gold medal for Jesse Owens!"

Matthew clapped his hands above his head, but then he saw what was happening down on the field.

Luz Long approached Jesse. At first Matthew worried, but to his surprise, Luz hugged Jesse. Matthew realized that maybe not everyone in Germany felt the same as Hitler. Luz seemed like a nice guy.

It was like that in America too. Lots of people were prejudiced, but not all of them.

Matthew realized he and Jesse had both won today. Matthew had beaten a bout with asthma, and Jesse won the long jump.

Tomorrow, maybe they could win again.

***

It had been a long night for Matthew. His father had warmed up some of Mama's nasty tea and made him drink another cup. Then he'd boiled one of Mama's other potions and made Matthew inhale the vapors.

Now Matthew was back in the press box waiting for the next event—the two-hundred-meter race. This was Jesse's last event of the games, and Matthew wanted him to make a clean sweep. Three gold medals would leave Jesse undefeated.

While Matthew waited, he eavesdropped on the reporters.

"You heard what the Nazi press is saying?" asked one.

"No, what?" asked another.

"They're saying America is only winning because of the Negroes," said the first one.

Matthew knew the Nazis were probably trying to insult the Negroes and the United States, but as far as he was concerned, it was a compliment. He felt proud that his people were doing a good job representing America. Maybe people would respect Negroes more after this.

Daddy clearly agreed. He interrupted the two men. "Well that means we must be as good as anyone else . . . or better."

Since the two reporters didn't answer Daddy, Matthew went right back to watching the warm-ups.

His father tapped his arm and asked, "How are you feeling?"

"Fine," answered Matthew. He hated to admit it, but Mama's medicines had helped. Maybe it wouldn't be long before he outgrew his sickness the same way Jesse had.

Matthew leaned closer to Daddy and whispered, "Hitler's not in his box today."

"I noticed," said Daddy. "I don't miss him any, though."

Matthew smiled and got to his feet. It was time for the two-hundred-meter race. This time, Jesse's biggest rival was someone on his own team—another Negro runner named Mack Robinson. Earlier in the games, Mack had been the first one to match Jesse's time.

Bang! The starter gun sounded, but this time Matthew didn't jump. He was used to it now. He knew that when *his* day to run in the Olympics came, he'd need to be ready to spring into action.

Jesse shot off his mark like a bullet out of a gun. It didn't look like his feet even touched the ground. Mack was on Jesse's trail, but not for long. Jesse took the lead and widened the gap between himself and the other runners.

Matthew balled up his fists and pumped his arms, just like Jesse.

"Take it easy, Matthew," Daddy reminded him gently.

But before Matthew's asthma could act up even a little bit, the race was over. Jesse had won the gold again!

"He did it, Daddy!" Matthew shouted. *"Three* golds! *Three!"*

Matthew took off his hat and waved it in the air as Jesse made his way to the winner's pedestal. Watching his hero compete was one thing, but watching him win every single event was another. It was a dream come true.

Matthew had to work hard to keep his excitement under control as they left the Olympic stadium at the end of the day. When the crowed thinned out, Matthew stopped in his tracks. He put one foot behind him and crouched.

"Bang!" he yelled. Then he took off as fast as he could down the street.

Matthew could hear Daddy yelling for him to slow down, but he ignored him. Nothing could stop him. He was Jesse Owens. He was a star. He was a three-time gold medal winner.

Matthew ran to the end of the block, and then he turned around and sprinted back to Daddy. When he got back to his father, he grinned.

"I wish Jesse had another race," Matthew said. "I wish there was just one more chance to watch him win."

Daddy put an arm around Matthew as they walked. "That would be exciting," he said. "But why don't we just enjoy the rest of the games?"

"Will Jesse Owens watch too?" Matthew asked.

"Yes," said Daddy. "He'll root for his team."

That was enough to satisfy Matthew. Just being in the same stadium as Jesse was exciting. They could root for America together.

Matthew wondered if Hitler would come back to root for his country tomorrow too.

Chapter 5

The Grand Finale

August 9, 1936
Olympic Stadium, Berlin, Germany

Matthew was ready to go back home. Rooting for the United States had been fun for a while, but the Olympics just weren't the same without Jesse running. And there were still five days of events left.

Matthew sat in the press box and watched the crowd. For some reason, there was a strange feeling in the stadium. To Matthew, it seemed like people were telling secrets.

"What's going on?" Matthew asked his father. "Why is everyone acting so funny?"

Daddy whispered, "Sounds like the coach is changing today's lineup."

"What coach? What lineup?" asked Matthew.

Daddy held his index finger up in the air. That was his signal for "just a minute." Matthew watched as his father looked around and listened to conversations.

Finally Daddy frowned and said, "The U.S. coach is pulling Stoller and Glickman out of the four-hundred-meter relay."

Another reporter asked, "Do you think it's because they're Jewish?"

Matthew's daddy shook his head and said, "I don't know why."

The reporters whispered and took notes. Everyone in the stadium waited to see what would happen next. Matthew watched the field. Jesse Owens was talking to the coach. They both had super-serious expressions on their faces.

Matthew felt sorry for Stoller and Glickman. He hoped they hadn't been taken out of the race for being Jewish. That wouldn't be fair at all.

Finally, Jesse walked toward the track. Ralph Metcalfe followed him.

"Jesse Owens!" yelled Matthew. "The coach is putting Jesse Owens and Ralph Metcalfe in the race!"

"That makes sense," said one of the reporters. "Might as well put in the fastest runners."

That would be a good reason to switch runners, Matthew thought. He hoped the reporter was right about the reason for the switch.

Matthew's eyes were glued to the track. He couldn't believe he would get to watch Jesse run again after all!

Everyone stood up as the American and Italian relay teams took their places on the track.

Matthew waited to see what order the relay team would run in. He thought it would be a good idea to put Jesse first or last. Then Jesse could either give the team a head start or make up the difference if they were behind at the end.

Jesse walked to the line where the first runner was supposed to start. That meant he would run the first leg of the race. The other three runners took their spots ahead of Jesse. Jesse would hand the baton off to Metcalfe, who would hand it to Foy Draper, who would give it to Frank Wykoff to finish the race.

The runners all stood on their marks. Jesse Owens and his team looked ready. Jesse put a leg back and crouched.

Matthew stood in position too and prepared for the pop of the gun. *Bang!*

Go! Matthew thought.

It looked as though Jesse didn't hesitate for even half a second when the gun fired. He sped off. Matthew knew it had been a good idea to put him first. Matthew watched as Ralph Metcalfe reached his hand back, ready for the handoff. Jesse ran to his teammate and gave him the baton. Metcalfe took off like a flash.

The handoff to Draper was smooth too, and Wykoff looked ready to finish the race. As soon as he had the baton, Wykoff ran as hard as he could. He ran the last leg like the boogeyman was chasing him.

"Go! Go! Go!" Matthew hollered.

It was like Wykoff could hear Matthew yelling. He sped to the finish line and won! As soon as he crossed the line, Matthew let out a loud cheer. The United States had won the gold medal again!

"Another world record," yelled the announcer. "The Americans win in thirty-nine point eight seconds! A one point three-second lead over their Italian rivals."

Thanks to Jesse's speed, they would be taking home a gold medal.

Matthew had never imagined he'd watch Jesse lead his country to *four* gold medals. He looked around the Olympic stadium. Matthew could tell he wasn't the only one who loved Jesse Owens. It seemed as if the whole world did.

If he can do this, I can too, thought Matthew. Then he threw his arms around his father. They hugged each other and jumped up and down at the same time.

The Olympics were a big win for Jesse Owens, but his victories were a win for other people too—for the team, the country, the Negro people, and of course, for Matthew.

Daddy let go of Matthew and held him at arm's length. "How do you feel?" he asked. "You okay?"

Matthew smiled. "I'm just fine," he said. And it wasn't even a lie.

THE HISTORY BEHIND JESSE OWENS'S OLYMPIC MEDALS

Many people know that Jesse Owens was a record-breaking Black track star on the 1936 U.S. Olympic team. What they might not know is how complicated things were that year. The American Olympians had to travel to Berlin, Germany, where the games were held. A lot of the athletes could barely afford to make the trip. At that time, the only way to get to Germany was by ship. That was very expensive. Jesse Owens was a student at Ohio State University in 1936. He managed to make the trip, but he only had one suit to wear and ten dollars in his pocket.

The German government also created problems both before and during the Olympics. Adolf Hitler ruled Germany as a dictator. He was a racist who especially hated Jewish people. He passed laws discriminating against them. He even banned Jewish athletes from the German Olympic teams. Things in Germany were so horrible that the United States considered boycotting the Olympics.

But there was also racism and prejudice in the United States. Black Americans were regularly faced with segregation and discrimination. Most of the Olympic athletes *wanted* to compete. They wanted to *win*. Black athletes, including Jesse Owens, saw the Olympics as a chance to show they were as good as anyone else. Ultimately, the U.S. decided to participate.

Jesse Owens did not seem likely to become an Olympic athlete. Born James Cleveland "J.C." Owens, he was very sickly as a boy. He often caught bad colds and once came down with pneumonia, a serious lung illness. His family lived in a shack with no heater. When J.C. was nine years old, his family moved north from Alabama to Ohio, hoping for a better life. His new teacher asked his name. "J.C.," he answered. The teacher thought he said Jesse. From then on, he was called Jesse.

Soon Jesse's speed was noticed by the junior high school track coach. Jesse ran track in junior high and high school. Later he received an offer to attend Ohio State University. There he was welcome on the team, but he couldn't live in the dorms because he was Black. Despite discrimination, Jesse broke five world records in forty-five minutes at the Big Ten College Championships. And then he was on the path to the Olympics, where he won four gold medals.

But Jesse returned home from the Olympics to more discrimination and segregation. He did not even receive congratulations for his gold medals from President Franklin D. Roosevelt. For many years, he struggled to make enough money to support his family.

These wrongs have since been addressed. In 1976, Jesse was awarded the Presidential Medal of Freedom by President Gerald Ford. In 1979, he received the Living Legend Award from President Jimmy Carter. Jesse Owens died of lung cancer in 1980, but has continued to be recognized. In 1984, a street in Berlin was named after him. His wife accepted the Congressional Gold Medal on his behalf in 1990. In 2001, Ohio State University named its stadium in Jesse Owens's honor.

ACTIVITY

Have Your Own Track and Field Event!

You can have fun with a simpler version of the Olympic 100-meter dash! Start with heats and move on to the finals, just like Jesse Owens.

What You Need:

- 7–12 runners (six runners fit on a track and wouldn't need a heat. More than 12 gets tricky.)

- a person who is not racing to be the recorder/timer (More than one can be helpful. It's hard for recorders to keep "track" of everyone.)

- an index card or slip of paper for each runner

- a clipboard and pencil

- a stopwatch or timer

- a track (If you can find a 100-meter track, that's great. If not, use the length of a football or soccer field. They are both very close to 100 meters.)

What to Do:

Step 1. Write each runner's name on a card or paper.

Step 2. Have each runner run the race alone. The recorder should time each person and record the time on their card. (Round the times to the nearest tenth—one number after the decimal.)

Step 3. Arrange the cards in order from fastest to slowest. Number them in order, with #1 being the fastest. Put the #1 card on the top of the pile and keep the cards in order.

Step 4. Split the cards into two groups for two heats by dealing the cards into two piles, the same way you do with playing cards. (One here, one there, one here, one there.)

Step 5. Have the first pile of runners run the first heat. The timer should add each runner's new time to his or her card.

Step 6. Repeat step 5 with the second group of runners for the second heat.

Step 7. Now it's time for the finals! The six runners with the fastest speeds in the heats will compete.

Step 8. Start the final race and record the speeds of each runner. Rank them from first to sixth place.

GLOSSARY

Aryan (AIR-ee-uhn)—a word Nazis used to describe Germans with blond hair and blue eyes, who were of a certain Christian religion

asthma (AZ-muh)—a condition that causes a person to wheeze and have difficulty breathing

boycott (BOY-kot)—to refuse to take part in something as a way of protesting

dictator (DIK-tay-tuhr)—a ruler who takes complete control of a country, often unjustly

discrimination (dis-kri-muh-NAY-shuhn)—unfair treatment of a person or group, often because of race, religion, gender, sexual orientation, or age

eavesdropped (EEVS-dropped)—listened secretly to a private conversation

impressed (ihm-PRESSED)—made someone think highly of you

Jewish (JOO-ihsh)—someone whose religion is Judaism, who is descended from Jewish people, or who participates in the culture surrounding Judaism

Nazi (NOT-zee)—a member of a political party that was led by Adolf Hitler; the Nazis ruled Germany from 1933 to 1945

Negro (NEE-groh)—a now out-of-date term for a Black American

prejudice (PRE-joo-dihss)—hatred or unfair treatment of people who belong to a particular group, such as a race or religion

press box (prehs boks)—a space reserved for reporters (as at a stadium)

segregation (seg-ruh-GAY-shuhn)—the practice of keeping groups of people apart, especially based on race

ABOUT THE AUTHOR

Nikki Shannon Smith is from Oakland, California, but she now lives in the Sacramento area with her family. She spends her days teaching elementary school and writes everything from picture books to young adult novels. Her books include *The Little Christmas Elf, Treasure Hunt.* For Capstone she has written The Amazing Life of Azaleah Lane series, and four books in the Girls Survive series. When she's not busy with family, work, or writing, Nikki loves to visit the Pacific Coast. The first thing she packs in her suitcase is always a book.

Nikki dedicates *A Star Like Jesse Owens* to her own son, Jesse, who makes her proud every day.

ABOUT THE ILLUSTRATOR

Lisa Manuzak Wiley is an illustrator and former video game concept artist. She was born and raised in Hawaii and loves bright colors, magic, and making people smile. She currently lives in southern California with her husband, their corgi, two fluffy kitties, and a lot of plants.